I'm waiting to see you in ballet shoes

To listen to your music and say,

your boyfriends or hear you say, "she's

wait is getting fun!   I want to read

afar. I can't believe I'm writing this,

or is it football pads?

"it's just a fad." I'm waiting to meet

the one."  Oh, unborn child, this

your poems and get postcards from

'cause I don't know who you are.

I Already Know

I LOVE YOU

This book, and an ocean of love, are for Jessica and Matt.
Special thanks to Louis S.
—E.S.

I Already Know I Love You
Text copyright © 2004 by Billy Crystal
Illustrations copyright © 2004 by Billy Crystal and Byron Preiss Visual Publications, Inc.
Manufactured in China.

Library of Congress Cataloging-in-Publication Data
Crystal, Billy.
I already know I love you / by Billy Crystal ; illustrated by Elizabeth Sayles. — 1st ed.
p.   cm.
Summary: A grandfather dreams of all the things he will do with his new grandchild.
ISBN-10: 0-06-059391-1 (trade bdg.) — ISBN-13: 978-0-06-059391-9 (trade bdg.)
ISBN-10: 0-06-059392-X (lib. bdg.) — ISBN-13: 978-0-06-059392-6 (lib. bdg.)
ISBN-10: 0-06-059393-8 (pbk.) — ISBN-13: 978-0-06-059393-3 (pbk.)
[1. Grandfathers—Fiction. 2. Babies—Fiction. 3. Stories in rhyme.] I. Sayles, Elizabeth, ill. II. Title.
PZ8.3.C88647Iae 2004   2003017609
[E]—dc22   CIP
                                                                                        AC

Typography by Jeanne L. Hogle
❖

It's one month till your arrival, and I don't know if you're girl or boy.
So I wanted this to be your first gift—sorry, it's not a toy.

For Ella Ryan, and the two beautiful souls you're named for.
—B.C.

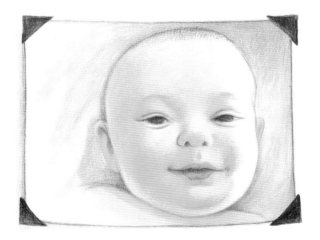

BILLY CRYSTAL

I Already Know
I LOVE
YOU

Illustrated by ELIZABETH SAYLES

HarperCollins*Publishers*

I'm going to be your grandpa!
I have the biggest smile.
I've been waiting to meet you
for such a long, long while.

I have so much to tell you
    before you slide into home plate.
I already know I love you
    as I sit right here and wait.

I'm waiting to show you everything,
hear your giggles and your sighs,
see butterflies and monkeys
and clowns who cross
their eyes.

I want to feel your heart beat
as you lie upon my chest,
bait your hook, fly your kite,
help you study for a test.

I'm waiting to play peekaboo...

and sing you to a nap.

I'm waiting to play horsey
and bounce you on my lap.

I'm waiting to show you the stars,
storm clouds, and the moon.
I want to make silly faces
and laugh just like a goon.

I want to show you the wind
and how it bends the grass.
I'm waiting to give you bear hugs—
the kind that last and last.

I'm waiting to show you oceans
and explain why the sky is blue.
I want to show you that lying
is never as good as true.

I can't wait to share spaghetti, wontons,
and ice-cream pie.

I can't wait to see your Brownie dress
and teach you how to tie.

I took your mom to her first movie.
   I want to take you, too.
That will be a special day
   devoted just to you.
When I took your mommy,
   I never watched the screen.
The movie was in her smile—
   to her it was a dream.

We'll go to see the Yankees,
    though your daddy loves the Sox.
I'm saving you signed baseballs—
    I keep them in a box.

I want to teach you about our family
   with pictures from long ago.
You're the new twig on our tree,
   and I can't wait to watch you grow.

Your mom is my daughter,
 and your dad is his mom's son.
You lived within your mommy,
 but now the time has come.
Get ready, little sweet one—
 your life will be just great.

I'm going to be your grandpa, and...

I can hardly wait.

I'm waiting to see you in ballet shoes

To listen to your music and say,

your boyfriends or hear you say,`she's

wait is getting fun!   I want to read

afar. I can't believe I'm writing this,

or is it football pads?

"it's just a fad."   I'm waiting to meet

the one."    Oh, unborn child, this

your poems and get postcards from

'cause I don't know who you are.